My Big Baby Brother

by Liza Charlesworth
illustrated by Joseph Wilkins

ISBN: 979-8-225-02081-1

Publisher: Tara Welty
Creative Director: Tannaz Fassihi; Designer: Cynthia Ng

1 2 3 4 5 6 7 8 9 10 68 34 33 32 31 30 29 28 27 26 25

Made in Jiaxing City, China. First printing, August 2025.

SCHOLASTIC

Hello! My name is Lenore and I am thirteen. Meet my baby brother, Hank. His age is one. Most of the time, Hank is sooooooo sweet. But if he gets too sleepy, it can be a nightmare. Got that? Good. Now, let me tell you about a very spooky thing that happened last night.

It all began when Mom asked me to babysit.
“Yippee!” I yelled. I like to babysit A LOT.
“I think you know all the rules,” said Mom.
“Hank gets a bath at four and a bottle at five.
Then you can sit and read him a little book.
Just get Hank in the crib by six on the dot.
If he misses his bedtime, he can be a beast.”

“Do not fret a bit. I got this!” I replied, as Mom grabbed her key ring and left. Yay! It was Hank time. We stacked blocks. We played patty-cake and peek-a-boo. After that, Hank walked across the room without falling. “Nice job!” I exclaimed.

Next came Hank's bath, followed by a bottle.
Then he sat on my lap with his stuffed cat
while I shared a book about a goofy banana.
The tale went on and on and on and on.
And when I checked the time—Oopsie!
The clock said it was one minute AFTER six.
So, I plopped Hank quickly in his crib.

A second later, a jagged bolt of lightning flashed across my brother's bedroom. Yikes! Things just did not feel right. Then I took a peek at Hank in his crib. His bright green eyes glowed and he started to get bigger and bigger and bigger. Eek! Hank had missed his bedtime at six and just as Mom said, he was turning into a beast!

Oh, my! I did not know what to do as Hank grew and grew and grew. SMASH, CRASH! He broke the bars of his crib and stomped out of his room, all the while screaming, "BOO-HOO, BOO-HOO, BOO-HOO!"

Quick as a wink, Hank was humongous!
In fact, he was about the size of a T. rex.
"What happened next?" you might ask.
Well, Hank tore off our nice front door
and stomped outside, crying and crying.
I felt bad that huge baby Hank was sad.

I knew I had made quite a mess of things. But I didn't have much time to think about it. Why? I needed to get Hank home—in a jiff! So, I grabbed his little stuffed cat and went after him. Where in the world was he going?

STOMP, STOMP, STOMP, STOMP!
For each step that Hank took, I took ten.
As Hank walked, he got bigger and bigger,
which made the folks in town scurry away.
“My, Hank has grown!” yelped Mrs. Potts.
“Yes, indeed! Run for your life!” I replied.

Dear me! Hank was a huge menace. He knocked down a swing set and stepped on a slide. CRASH, SMASH! Then he picked up a tree and ate it—as if it were broccoli. CHOMP, CHOMP! "At least he's getting his veggies," I said.

STOMP, STOMP, STOMP, STOMP!
Hank was just not in his right mind.
His eyes glowed like two green lights.
Then he turned around to face the lake
and spotted a sailboat on the waves.
He walked toward it. SPLISH, SPLASH!
"Noooooooo!" I screamed. "Hank thinks
the boat is a toy for him to play with."

Good news! A siren blared and a red fire truck parked at Hank's chubby feet. "Hank, put that boat back on the lake!" said fireman Steve on his megaphone. At first, Hank did just as he was told. But then, he picked up the fire truck!

Now, it was my turn to spring into action. I grabbed the megaphone and yelled, "Hank, that fire truck is real, not a toy. Place it on the ground and look at this!" Then I held up his teeny tiny stuffed cat. Would he put down the truck and grab it?

To tell the truth, I don't have an answer. The next thing I knew, Mom was poking me and saying: "Time to wake up, Lenore. It is ten o'clock and I just got back home. Thanks for taking such good care of Hank. He's sound asleep with a happy smile."

Wait a sec. What the heck was going on?
I pinched myself and it hurt—quite a bit!
Then I took a peek at baby Hank in his crib.
Mom was right. He gripped his stuffed cat
as he slept like a sweet little angel.
What a huge relief! My big baby brother . . .
was just a spooky dream.